A Sitter for Baby Monster

SESAME STREET

A GROWING-UP BOOK ™

By Emily Perl Kingsley
Illustrated by Tom Cooke

Featuring Jim Henson's Sesame Street Muppets

A SESAME STREET / GOLDEN PRESS BOOK
Published by Western Publishing Company, Inc., in conjunction with Children's Television Workshop.

One Monday morning Flossie's mommy sat down on the edge of Flossie's bed to tell her something important.

"I am going to work today," said Mommy. "Remember when I told you about my new job? I am a teacher, and today is the first day of school."

"Am I going to work with you?" asked Flossie.

"No," said Mommy as she helped Flossie get dressed. "You may not come to work with me. Your baby-sitter, Dolores, is coming to stay with you. She has stayed with you before. You remember I told you she'd be coming today?"

"I don't want a baby-sitter," said Flossie. "I want you to stay home with me."

"I can't stay home, because I have to go to work," explained Mommy. "But you always have a good time with Dolores. She takes good care of you."

The doorbell rang.

"There she is now," said Mommy. "Let's go let her in."

"Hello, Dolores," said Mommy. "Come in."

"Hi, Flossie!" said Dolores. "How are you? I brought some pictures of my cat, Ralph. Remember when I told you about him? One day we'll go to my house so you can play with him."

Mommy wrote a list and put it up on the refrigerator.
"Here is my phone number at work, in case you need to
reach me," she said. "And here is the number of Flossie's
doctor...and our neighbor monster next door...and other
emergency numbers."

"Okay, thanks," said Dolores.

Then Mommy showed Dolores where to find everything
that a baby monster would need.

"Oh," said Mommy, "Flossie always wears her pink
sneakers when she goes to the park."

Mommy hugged Flossie good-bye. "You have a good time with Dolores, and I'll see you after work."

"Do you promise you'll come home?" asked Flossie.

"Of course," said Mommy. "I always come home. I'll be home in time for dinner. Now give Mommy a big kiss."

And Mommy went to work.

Flossie stood at the window and watched Mommy walk down the sidewalk. Mommy waved good-bye. Flossie waved back.

"Would you like to see the pictures of Ralph now?" Dolores asked Flossie.

Dolores and Flossie sat on the
sofa and looked at the pictures
of Ralph.

Then they moved the furniture
around in Flossie's dollhouse and
put together a puzzle.

They built a fort
with Flossie's blocks.
"Mommy always helps
me build it up and
then lets me crash
the tower down,"
said Flossie.

"That sounds like fun,"
said Dolores. So they
built lots of tall buildings
and crashed them down.
"Now let's put everything
away," said Dolores.

Dolores made Flossie a monster-burger for lunch.
"Mommy always puts my ketchup on the side of my
monster-burger," said Flossie. "You put it on top. I don't
like it on top."
"I didn't know that," said Dolores. "Why don't you try
it and see how it tastes this way."
Flossie took a small bite. Then she ate the rest.

"Mommy always gives me a straw for my milk," said
Flossie.

Dolores looked around the kitchen until she found
the straws. Then she put one into Flossie's glass of milk.

"Here you are," she said.

"Thank you," said Flossie.

Dolores smiled.

GOOD NIGHT MONSTER

After lunch, Dolores read Flossie's favorite book, *Good Night, Monster.*

"I don't want to take a nap," Flossie told Dolores.

"Oh, you don't have to go to sleep," said Dolores. "Just lie down and rest for a while."

"Mommy always sings me a song," said Flossie.

"I can sing you a song, too," said Dolores.

"Mommy sings me 'Rockabye, Monster.'"

Dolores sang "Rockabye, Monster" to Flossie.

"Mommy sings it different," said Flossie, "but your way is pretty good, too."

Then Dolores sang another song. She sang "Hush, Little Monster, Don't Say a Word."

By the end of the song, Flossie was fast asleep.

When Flossie woke up from her nap, Herry came home from play group.

"Hi, Dolores!" said Herry. "May I please have some Monster Crunch cookies with my milk?"

Herry and Flossie had a snack. Then Dolores said, "I have a great idea. It's a beautiful day. Let's go to the park."

"Since I'm the big brother," said Herry, "may I hold Flossie's hand when we cross the street?"

"Since I'm the monster-sitter," said Dolores, "please hold one of my hands while Flossie holds the other. Then we'll cross the street."

When they got to the park, the first thing Flossie did was push Teddy Monster in the swing. Then Herry pushed Flossie in the swing. Then Dolores pushed them both.

"Higher!" shouted Herry.

"Higher!" shouted Flossie.

Then Dolores caught them
when they came down the slide.

She helped Flossie balance on
the seesaw.

In the sandbox Herry made a road for his truck.

"I want to push the truck," said Flossie.

"No, I'm playing with it," said Herry.

They both tugged at the truck until one of the wheels came off.

"Now look what you did," said Herry. "You broke the truck. I'm going to tell Mommy!"

"Listen, little monsters," said Dolores, "you must take turns with the truck." Dolores put the wheel back on the truck. "Here's a shovel, Flossie. Why don't you dig in the sand until it's your turn to play with the truck."

On the way home from the park they stopped at Mr. McIntosh's vegetable stand.

"Let's buy some apples," said Dolores.

"I want to choose them," said Herry.

"Mommy always lets me pick out the apples," said Flossie.

"Herry," said Dolores. "You pick three apples, and Flossie will pick three apples."

"Then we'll have six," said Herry.

At home again, Dolores said, "Let's set the table so it will be ready for dinner when Mommy and Daddy come home from work."

"We never did that before," said Flossie.

They set four places. Herry put the plates and the forks on the table. Flossie put the spoons and the napkins on either side of the plates. Dolores added the knives and the glasses.

When Mommy and Daddy arrived home from work at the end of the day, Flossie and Herry ran to kiss them hello.

"Oh, my goodness," said Daddy. "Who set the table?"

"We did! We did!" cried Herry and Flossie.

"What a wonderful surprise," said Mommy.

"We did it all by ourselves...with Dolores," said Flossie.

That night, as Mommy tucked Flossie into bed, Flossie told her all about the day with Dolores.

"Is Dolores coming again tomorrow?" asked Flossie.

"Yes," said Mommy. "She will come every day when I go to work."

Then Mommy sang "Rockabye, Monster" to Flossie.

"Mommy," asked Flossie at the end of the song, "do you know 'Hush, Little Monster, Don't Say a Word'?"